Usborne Activities

100 Things
to do on a
Plane

Sam Smith

Illustrated by Non Figg
and Molly Sage

Designed by Michael Hill

Edited by Sam Taplin

D0029336

Packing jumble

Ryan's room is a mess. Look for all the items on his packing list, then underline the item that isn't there.

Packing list:
camera
2 T-shirts
toothbrush
beach ball
pair of goggles
purple shorts
sunglasses
sunscreen
sunhat
snorkel and mask
bottle of water

Key match-up

Circle the two sets of keys that can be turned so that they match each other exactly.

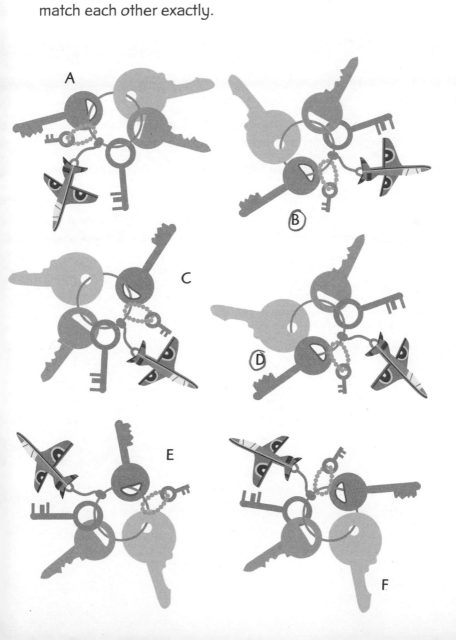

From the air

Help the green car take the quickest route to the airport, avoiding the tractors and any other obstacles.

Forward and back

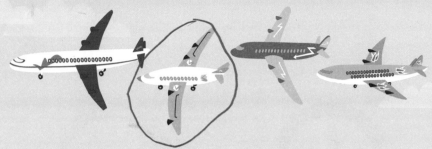

1. Circle the plane in front of the plane that is two behind the plane in front of the plane behind the red plane.

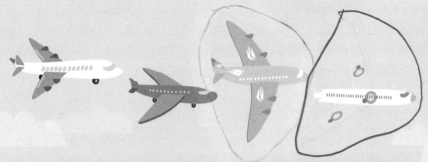

2. Circle the plane two in front of the plane in front of the plane three behind the plane in front of the green plane.

3. Circle the car that's two in front of the car two behind the car in front of the car in front of the blue car.

Time zones

The time in London is nine hours behind the time in Sydney. Madrid is five hours behind Beijing and six hours ahead of Boston. Dubai is three hours ahead of London. Write each city's name under the correct clock.

LONDON

Air quiz

1) What was the name of the first powered plane?
a) Bumblebee   b) Flyer   c) Albatross

2) Who, in Greek myth, flew too close to the Sun?
a) Daedalus   b) Apollo   c) Icarus

3) What did Han Solo fly in *Star Wars*?
a) Death Star   b) *Millennium Falcon*   c) TIE fighter

4) A plane's 'black box' flight recorder is usually...
a) orange   b) black   c) green

5) Which of these was a famous flying ace in WW1?
a) Blue Duke   b) Purple Prince   c) Red Baron

6) The pilots of an airliner never eat the same meal as each other. True or false?

7) Who flies in a plane called Air Force One?
a) U.S. President   b) the Pope   c) Bill Gates

Parking space

The blue car that's just arriving has a reserved parking space between two other cars that are the same model as it, but not necessarily the same shade. Find the space and circle it.

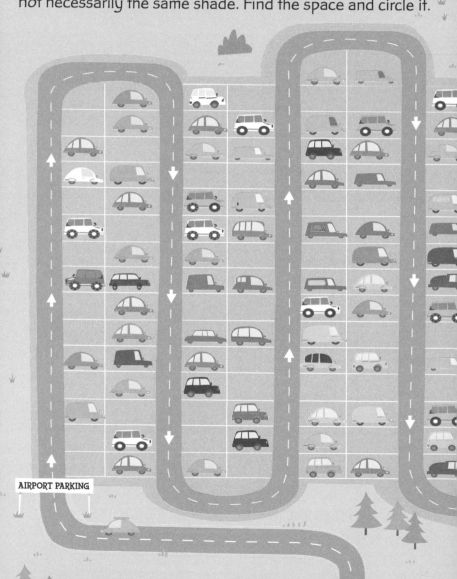

AIRPORT PARKING

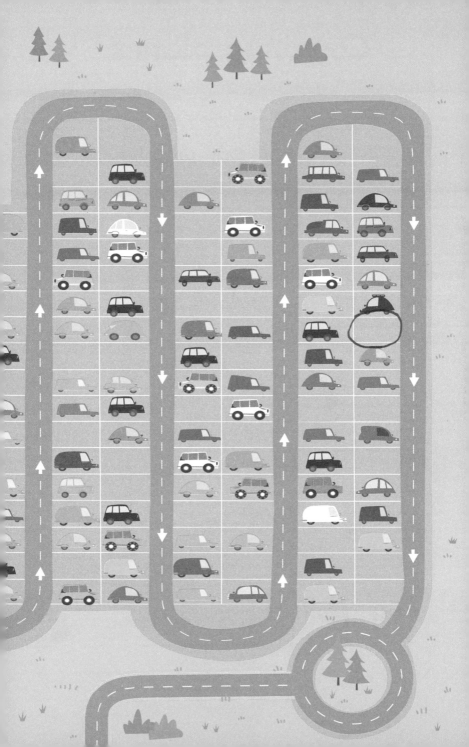

Counting planes

On Friday, Sam counted 56 planes to help him fall asleep.
He counted half as many on Saturday, and then each
night for the rest of the week he counted three fewer than
the night before. How many planes did Sam count on
Thursday night? Use the space below for any calculations
you may want to do.

$$28$$
$$2\overline{)56}$$
$$-4$$
$$16$$
$$16$$
$$0$$

S 25
M 22
T 19
W 16
T 13

ANSWER 13

Loading luggage

Steer the baggage truck along a clear path to the plane waiting at the bottom.

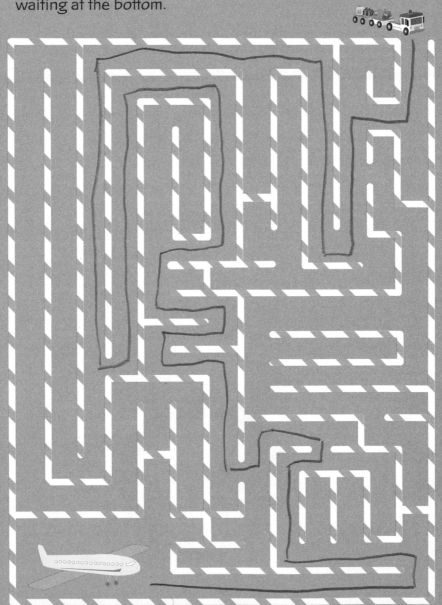

10

Anna's alarm

Anna is catching a morning flight to Los Angeles. Use the information below to find out what time she needs to set her alarm for. Draw the clock hands to show your answer.

She needs 15 minutes to have a shower.

Having breakfast will take ten minutes.

It takes an hour and a half to get to the airport.

She has to check in two hours before her flight departs.

Her flight leaves at 08:30.

Draw a plane

Follow the steps below to draw a plane, then add more of them flying above the clouds.

1. Draw a long cabin and two wings.

2. Add engines and the tail.

3. Draw lots of windows.

Bags and cases

A group of people are waiting at the check-in desk. Altogether, they have ten pieces of luggage.

- They have two red bags and one red suitcase.
- They have one more red bag than blue bags.
- They have one more green suitcase than red suitcases.
- The number of orange bags is equal to the number of blue bags and the number of green suitcases added together. The rest of the bags are yellow.

How many items of luggage are:

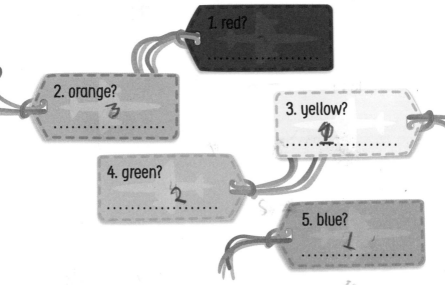

1. red?

2. orange?
3

3. yellow?
1

4. green?
2

5. blue?
1

Use this space for any calculations you may want to do:

Symbol sudoku

This grid is made up of six blocks, each made up of six squares. Fill in the blank squares so that every row, column and block contains all six airport symbols shown below.

Flag mix-up

Unscramble the country names on the right, then match each one to the correct flag.

un ited states
DUNTIE TASSET

Germany
MANGERY

mexico
ECOMIX

France
CANFER

New zealand
WEN ANDLAZE

Jamaica
CAJIAMA

Lost luggage

Draw along the strings to match the luggage labels to the correct bags.

Departures

Use the departures board to answer the questions below.

Time	To	Flight	Gate
✈	**DEPARTURES**		**T1**
08:35	NEW YORK	QWE142	11
08:50	VENICE	ERT364	17
09:05	PARIS	ASD332	05
09:10	BARCELONA	VBN112	01
09:15	MILAN	GHJ987	21
09:15	SYDNEY	HJY756	31
09:25	BERLIN	RTW444	29
09:35	FLORENCE	DFG175	03
09:40	MADRID	UPL645	08
09:55	CAIRO	HHT352	16
09:55	AMSTERDAM	QVF376	11
10:00	ROME	AXF285	05

1. Joe's flying to Italy some time after 08:50. He's not going to the capital and his gate is a prime number. Which flight is his?

ANSWER ...DFG175...

2. Alice is going to visit Notre Dame and the Louvre during her city break. What time is the flight she needs to catch?

ANSWER .....9:05.....

Flight plan

Which way should the pilot fly to Chocksville?
She can only switch flight paths at a fuel stop,
and needs the route with just seven stops
along the way.

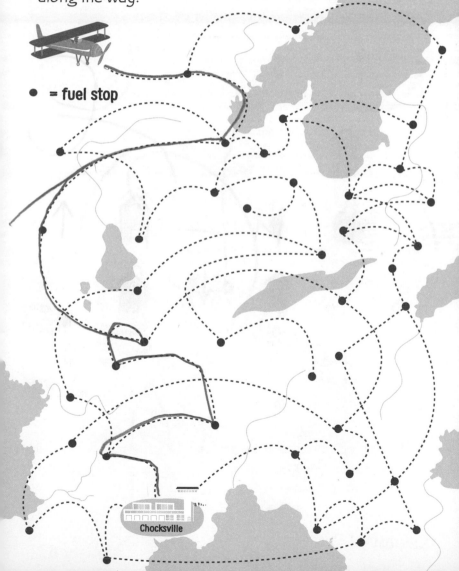

● = fuel stop

Chocksville

Planes puzzle

Four planes take off from the same airport on the same day.

* The first plane returns to the airport once a day.
* The second plane returns every other day.
* The third plane returns every three days.
* The fourth plane returns every four days.

If they take off late at night on day 1, which is the next day when all four planes are due back at the airport together?

ANSWER ..12..............

Cross sum

Fill in the blank squares with numbers from 1 to 9 so that the numbers in each row and column add up to the total shown on its plane. (The direction of the planes shows you whether to add across or down the grid.) You can only use a number once in an answer. For example, you can make 4 with 3 and 1, but not with 2 and 2.

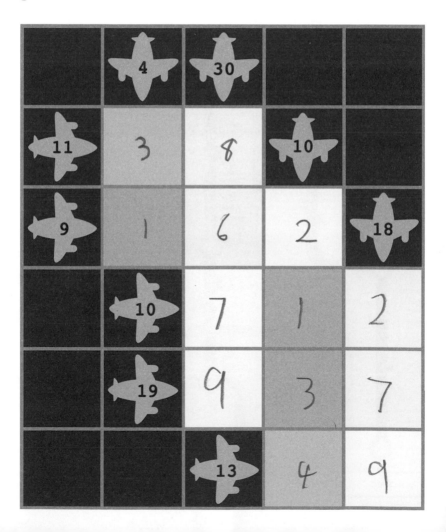

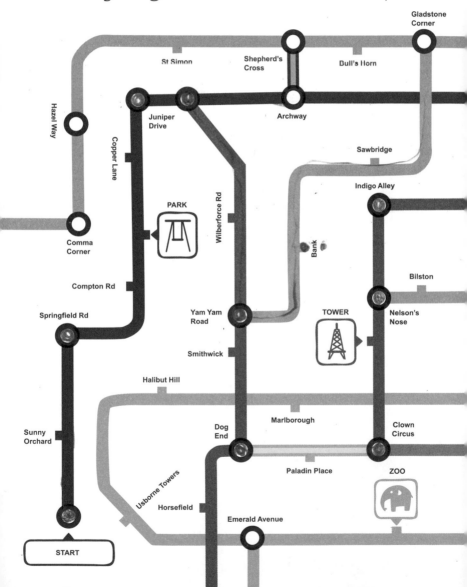

Hotel hurry

Lisa needs to get to the airport via her hotel in Bank. Find both on the underground map and plan her shortest route. She can only change to a different line at a circle stop.

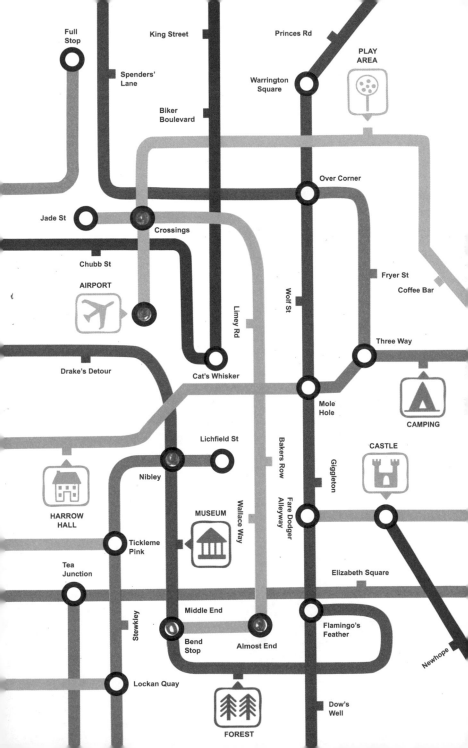

Full
Stop

King Street

Princes Rd

PLAY
AREA

Spenders'
Lane

Warrington
Square

Biker
Boulevard

Over Corner

Jade St

Crossings

Fryer St

Coffee Bar

Chubb St

Wolf St

AIRPORT

Three Way

Limey Rd

CAMPING

Drake's Detour

Mole
Hole

Cat's Whisker

CASTLE

Lichfield St

Bakers Row

Giggleton

Nibley

HARROW
HALL

Fare Dodger
Alleyway

Tickleme
Pink

MUSEUM

Wallace Way

Elizabeth Square

Tea
Junction

Middle End

Flamingo's
Feather

Stewkley

Bend
Stop

Almost End

Newhope

Lockan Quay

Dow's
Well

FOREST

Gridlock

Lauren and Ethan are stuck in traffic near the airport. Lauren looks out of her window and sees 4 blue cars, 6 red cars, and 10 green cars. Ethan looks out of his window and sees 12 green cars, 6 red cars, 4 blue cars, and 2 black cars.

What percentage of Lauren's cars are blue? 20%

What percentage of Ethan's cars are red? 25%

What percentage of all the cars both can see are green? 50%

Flying machines

Doodle on these shapes to turn them into flying machines.

Pack your bag

Draw lots of things you want to take with you on your trip.

Quick draw

Draw a line as fast as you can from the plane to the end of its trail, without touching the sides.

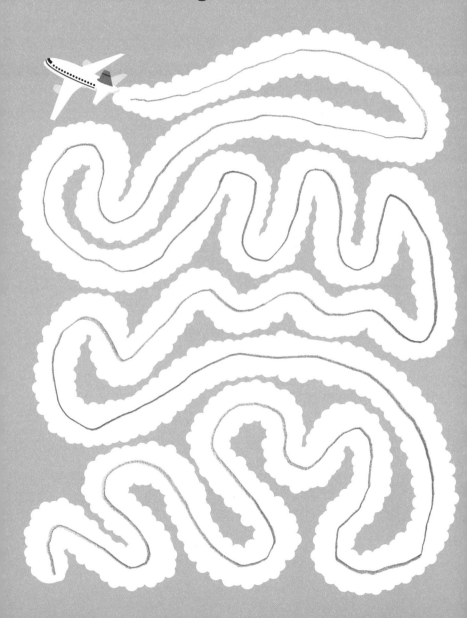

Outside the airport

Draw some more planes in the sky outside the airport.

What am I?

1. I always run, but never walk.
I always murmur, but never talk.
I have a bed but do not sleep.
I have a mouth but do not eat.

river

2. I can fly but I have no wings. I can cry but I have no eyes. Wherever I go, darkness follows me.

cloud

3. I have a face, but no eyes.
I have hands but no arms.

clock

4. I'm lighter than a feather, but even the strongest person can't hold me for long.

breath

5. I start with 'E' and end with 'E', and inside me there's a letter.

envelope

arrow

6. I have feathers that help me fly,
I have a head but I'm not alive.
My journey's length depends on strength.

7. I travel around the world, but always stay in one corner.

Stamp

Excess baggage

The maximum weight of luggage a small plane can carry is 150 units. The number of units each item weighs is written on its label. Which one must the plane leave behind?

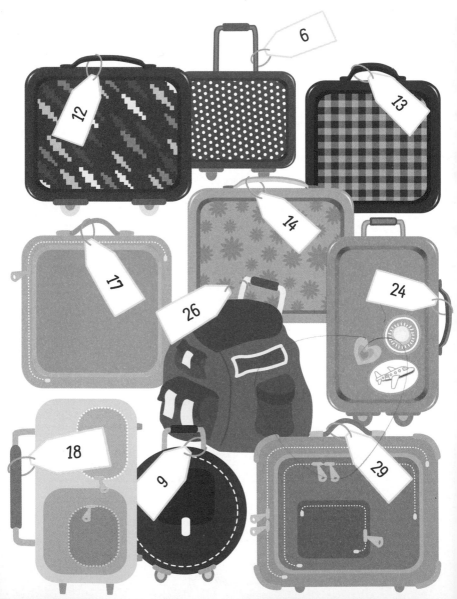

Globe words

How many names of **real** countries can you find among the words on the globe below?

BONECHINADOLLNARNIA
SWEDENRUSHERRORGREASE
CREATEISLANDEGYPTCANADATAPED
CHILLYCOLONYPOLANDNORWAYPANIC
PLUMPROMANIARIVERVILLAINCOSTARICA
BIRDLANDTURKEYNATIVECASHEWAGILITYAGO
TROPICOCEANMADAGASCARBRAZILINCASON
MAGENTAIRELANDBANANANETHERLANDSPOT
JAMAICAKNOWNINJAPANHUNGRYSAXONCHILE
PORTUGALVENTFIJIRUSSIAGONEPROVINCE
ALMONDPACIFICPERUSEATICELANDWAIT
BEAROUTFRANCELILLIPUTRAFTITALY
NEVERLANDINDIAGUITARMEXCO
TWOMANGERMANYCOLDER

Plane scramble

Can you unscramble these letters to find the names of six things you might find on a plane?

tailuptoo = ...

picktoc = ...

gannild rage = ...

dresswaste = ...

greensaps = ...

antpica = ...

Flight timeline

Label these flying inventions with numbers 1 to 6 to put them in order of their first flights, using 1 for the earliest.

Helicopter . . . . .

Hot-air balloon . . . . .

Plane . . . . .

Glider . . . . .

Space Shuttle . . . . .

Kite . . . . .

31

Stunt planes

The stunt planes below are flying in formation. Draw arrows to show how the triangle they're in can be turned upside down by just three of the planes changing position.

Crossword 1

Use the clues below to put the correct words into the grid.

¹C	o	²n	o	o	³r	d	⁴e
l		a			a		a
o		⁵g	l	i	d	e	r	s
u					a		l
⁶d	a	⁷y		⁸P	r	⁹e	y
		e			c		
¹⁰s	t	a	r	¹¹s	¹²h	a	¹³t
a		r		e	o		r
¹⁴d	i	s	m	a	l	¹⁵b	y

Across

1. Supersonic passenger plane (8)
5. Unpowered planes (7)
6. 24 hours (3)
8. An eagle is a bird of _____ (4)
10. They shine in the night sky (5)
12. You wear it on your head (3)
14. Dreary, gloomy (6)
15. Next to (2)

Down

1. White shape in the sky (5)
2. Hassle (3)
3. A plane uses it to know its own location (5)
4. Opposite of late (5)
7. Periods of 12 months (5)
9. A reflected sound (4)
10. Unhappy (3)
11. Large body of water (3)
13. Attempt (3)

Air race

Five planes were in a race. *Lightning* finished before *Pinky* but after *Phantom*. *Rainbow* wasn't first, but finished two places in front of *Camouflage*. No plane beginning with 'P' finished last. Write the correct finishing position on each of the planes.

Aircraft search

Find the aircraft below hidden in the grid.
They may be written in any direction.

airship

rocket

drone

glider

helicopter

blimp

balloon

biplane

jet

R	D	G	L	I	D	E	R	G	L
E	P	B	O	P	T	E	O	R	N
T	C	S	I	T	E	K	C	O	R
P	E	B	H	P	J	F	O	C	Y
O	M	J	S	Y	L	L	B	R	D
C	G	I	G	P	L	A	B	V	E
I	A	U	L	A	C	T	N	G	N
L	U	L	B	B	M	W	V	E	O
E	P	I	H	S	R	I	A	G	R
H	C	D	H	I	T	R	U	I	D

Cities in the sky

Each balloon has half a famous city's name on it. Draw lines between the correct balloons to complete each city's name.

BON

LIN

NEY

LON

LIS

COW

ATH

DON

MOS

BER

SYD

ENS

Travel times

Travel times

Use the information below to find out how long each of the flights took. Then, write down which was the longest flight and which was the shortest.

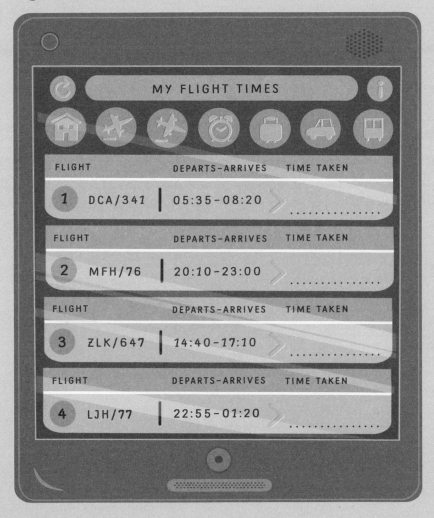

MY FLIGHT TIMES

FLIGHT	DEPARTS–ARRIVES	TIME TAKEN
1 DCA/341	05:35 – 08:20	
2 MFH/76	20:10 – 23:00	
3 ZLK/647	14:40 – 17:10	
4 LJH/77	22:55 – 01:20	

Longest flight: ....   Shortest flight: ....

Lines and dots

Fill in all the dotted shapes to find out what's concealed below.

Hot-air balloon

How many times each do the words HOT and AIR appear in the grid below? They may be written in any direction.

```
  I O H T I
 A I T I A R A
I T O R O R T I I
R H H I H I T O A O R
O H A H A O A I I T H
A I O I H R T T R O T
T I H T I A T A T R O
T R A I T O R H A
 H I O I H T I
  R I A R T
   T O H
```

HOT . . . .   AIR . . . .

Around the airport

A plane is about to land at this bustling airport. Can you guide it safely from the runway to the front of Terminal One? Be careful, some of the routes are blocked.

TERMINAL 1

Find your bag

Fortunately your bag is slightly different from all of the others here. Can you find and circle it?

Landmarks quiz

1) Which civilization built Stonehenge?

a) Romans   b) Ancient Greeks   c) Ancient Britons

2) The Empire State Building is the tallest building in the world. True or false?

3) The Statue of Liberty was a gift to the United States from which country?

a) Britain   b) France   c) Russia

4) The Great Sphinx is a statue that guards...

a) The Pyramids of Giza

b) The Terracotta Army

c) The Acropolis

5) What type of building is the Taj Mahal?

a) a tomb   b) a temple   c) a fortress

6) Where are the faces of four U.S. presidents carved into a cliff face?

a) Ayers Rock

b) Yellowstone

c) Mount Rushmore

Plane mechanic

Mike the mechanic has got two hours to service one of the planes below. It takes him ten minutes to get some spark plugs from the depot and five minutes to find a wrench for the wheel nuts. Which plane has he got time to repair?

OFFICIAL PLANE SERVICING DOCUMENT

PLANE	REPAIRS REQUIRED – TIME NEEDED
1	Tune engine – 50 minutes Change one wheel – 45 minutes General inspection – 30 minutes
2	Change plugs – 20 minutes Change two wheels – 90 minutes General inspection – 30 minutes
3	Repair wing flap – 45 minutes Tune engine – 50 minutes General inspection – 30 minutes
4	Change plugs – 20 minutes Change one wheel – 45 minutes General inspection – 30 minutes

Matching flags

Each of these flags is identical to one of the others.
Number each matching pair.

Flight chart

A pilot flies five types of planes – Boeing 737, Airbus A380, Antonov AN-158, Learjet 60, and Beechcraft 1900. He draws a chart to show how many times he flew each type in one month, but forgets to write down their names. He knows he flew a Boeing 737 once more than an Airbus 380, and an Antonov AN-158 the same number of times as a Learjet 60.

How many times did he fly each type of plane?

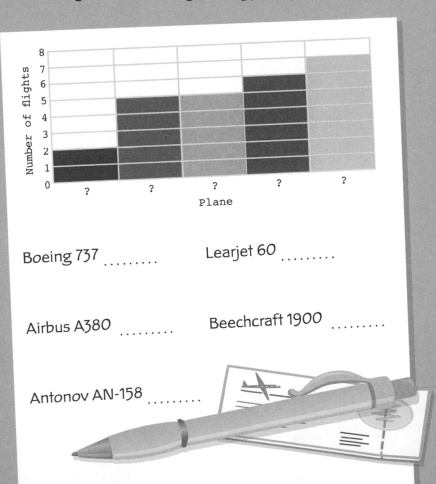

Boeing 737 ....   Learjet 60 ....

Airbus A380 ....   Beechcraft 1900 ....

Antonov AN-158 ....

Draw a helicopter

Follow the steps below to draw a helicopter, then add more of them hovering in the sky.

1. Draw these two shapes.

2. Join them, and add a landing skid.

3. Add the rotor blades, like this.

4. Draw windows and an 'X' in the circle.

Earth splitting

The flight path of the plane below has divided the Earth into two parts. Try to split the Earth into **seven** parts by drawing just two more straight lines.

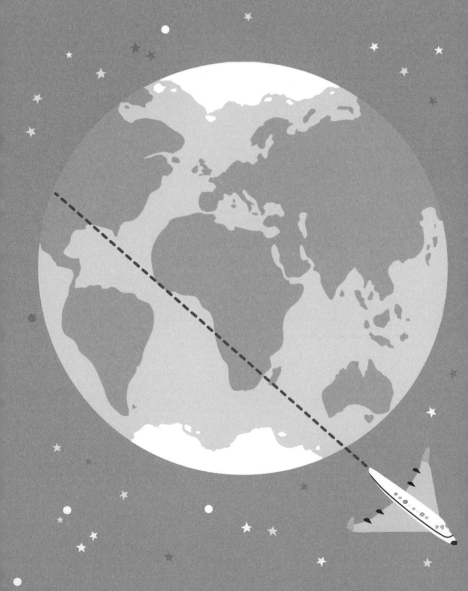

Crossnumber

Use the clues below to put the correct numbers into the grid.

Across ✈

1. Wings on 6,076 jumbo jets
3. Unlucky number?
5. *Around the World in ___ Days*
6. Last year of World War Two
9. James Bond's codename
11. Legs on 57 spiders
13. 90 divided by 6
14. 'Maximum' break in snooker
16. Days in a leap year
17. 2125 minus 141

Down ✈

1. ___ *Dalmatians*
2. Days in February
4. Degrees in a circle
7. Hogwart's Express platform number written as a decimal
8. States in the U.S.A.
10. 516 + 231
12. 9,003 minus 2,929
13. The first three numbers
15. 4 down + 51

Cloud shapes

Doodle on the clouds to turn them into interesting things, like the lion and the crocodile below.

True or false?

T/F

1. Modern passenger planes can fly all the way around the world without stopping.

T/F

2. The shortest commercial flight lasts just two minutes.

T/F

3. The inventors of the first powered plane built and repaired bicycles for a living.

T/F

4. A plane's autopilot is often nicknamed George.

T/F

5. More jets land in New York each year than in any other city.

T/F

6. Floating spiders have been known to land on weather balloons high above the clouds.

T/F

7. Airliners are designed so that they can survive being struck by lightning.

Items of luggage

Draw lots more items to take with you on your family trip.

On autopilot

Pilot Pete has set the autopilot to guide the plane on the short flight from Wells to Mayfield. The programmed path includes exactly six turns. Can you draw the route on the screen below?

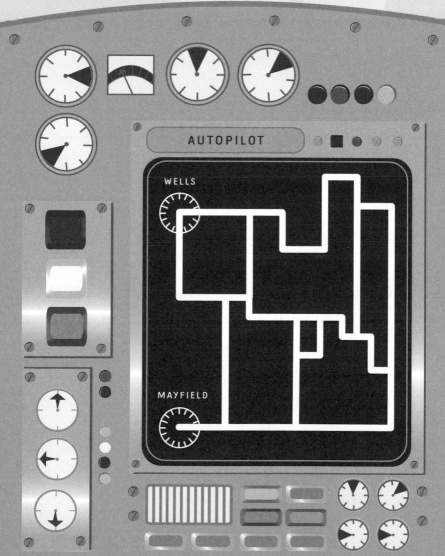

Radio alphabet

When they're talking on their radio, pilots use the words below to stand for the letters they begin with. For example, Romeo is R. Find all of the words of the radio alphabet in the grid below. They may be written in any direction.

Alpha Bravo Charlie Delta Echo Foxtrot

Zulu Yankee X-ray Golf Hotel

```
y s w o s c a r o h c e
y t e i l r a h c v e p
a e e v g y a n k e e d
h x k i r e b m e v o n
p o p s l d i y c b d m
l f x a i u l a y r c r
a o o q p h j r t e u o
r z t x l a w x b l l f
o s u k t r s e e i n i
m a i l i r u t m a b n
e i c e u q o a o t r u
o d f v r h m t q l a o
p n m l u r r i b e v l
v i c t o r a c k d o i
b r s o o g n a t e c k
```

Whiskey India Victor Juliet Uniform Kilo Tango Lima Sierra Mike Quebec Romeo Papa Oscar November

Takeoff doodle

Fill the page with lots more trees and fields, and anything else you might see as the plane leaves the ground.

Ground control

Look at the code below, then follow the directions to guide each plane to the correct terminal.

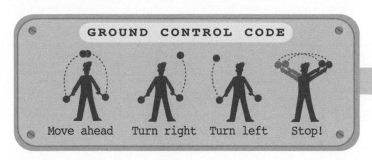

GROUND CONTROL CODE

Move ahead   Turn right   Turn left   Stop!

Red plane

Blue plane

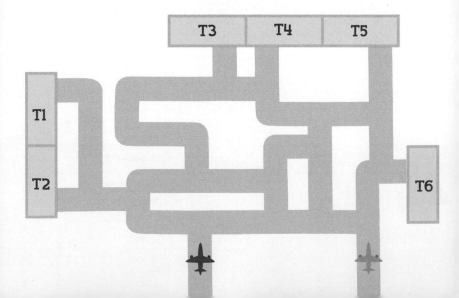

Plane designs

Draw spots on 20% of the blank plane outlines below.
Then, draw squares on 25% of the planes left blank.
Next, draw stripes on 1/3 of the planes that are blank.
Lastly, draw swirls on 1/4 of the blank planes.

How many planes are
left blank?

ANSWER
. . . .

Runway rules

Find out what the planes on each runway have in common, then choose the plane that follows each rule. Write their letters in the empty signs.

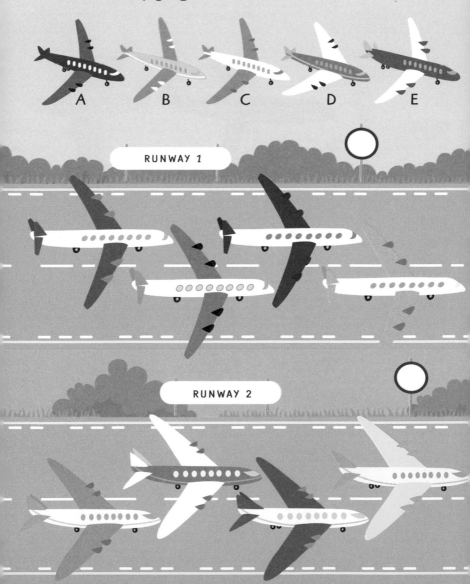

Stunt search

Find the names of the aerobatic stunts below hidden
in the grid. They may be written in any direction.

```
E S U R W I N W O V R N
T D A E H R E M M A H P
L Y S S R E V O R O K S
O L A Z Y E I G H T C O
R R O O L O O W A I A T
I E U R L R T Y S V B A
M Z V I T P O S L I H R
A T A O I G O A R D C M
L R L D G R Z O B E T M
H P I W S N N K L I I A
A V G E R I I C Y G P H
E B E S P I N W Z H T K
```

roll

scissors

pitchback

hammerhead

loop

dive

wingover

spin

lazy eight

Birds in words

Can you find these names of birds hidden in the sentences below? The first one has already been done for you.

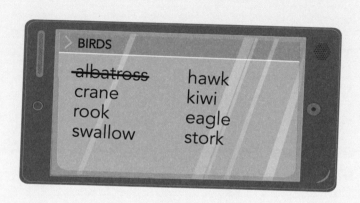

> BIRDS

~~albatross~~   hawk
crane   kiwi
rook   eagle
swallow   stork

1. The usual bat Ross uses is broken.

2. The republic ran everything after that.

3. Sam learned to ski with his parents.

4. The kangaroo kicked his rival hard.

5. Alice climbed the path awkwardly in her heels.

6. The sea gleamed in the sunshine.

7. We can either go West, or keep going North.

8. The man who built this wall owns the land.

Flying jumble

How many flying objects can you count in the jumbled shapes below?

Crossword 2

Use the clues below to put the correct words into the grid.

Across

1. Worldwide (6)
5. The end of a wing (3)
7. Time between birth and death (4)
8. Sit on water without sinking (6)
9. Sticky covering for roads (3)
10. Rescued; kept for later (5)
11. Curved structure (4)
12. Mythical fire bird (7)
14. Opposite of West (4)
15. Fire-breathing beasts (7)

Down

2. Bird that hunts at night (3)
3. He owned a magic lamp (7)
4. Illuminated; started (a fire) (3)
5. Tie down (rhymes with 8 down) (6)
6. A skydiver uses one (9)
8. Part of plumage; a quill (7)
11. Choppers (4)
13. What 2 down comes from (3)

Flags scramble

Unscramble the country names on the left, then match each one to the correct flag.

THUSO CAIRAF

ISATLAURA

YALTI

NACAAD

ZIBLAR

WANDSZITREL

Airline dinner

What's on the menu for today's in-flight dinner? Draw your ideal meal on the tray.

PEPPER

SALT

Hidden picture

Fill in all the shapes that contain numbers that can be divided by three. What can you see?

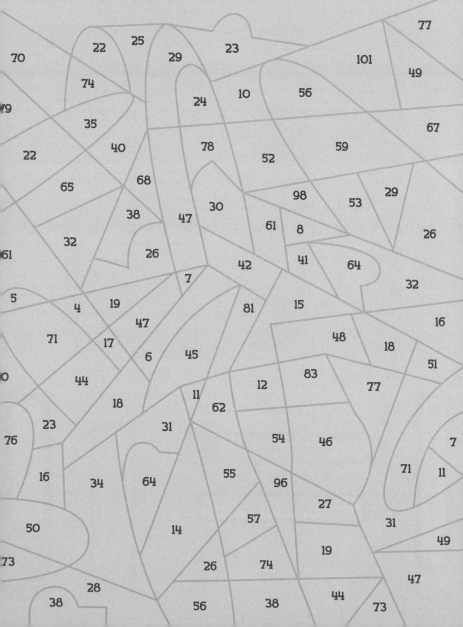

Capital cities

Look at the books below. Draw lines matching each country to the name of its capital city, then search for all the words in the grid. They may be written in any direction.

```
P D C C U C S P A I M G
C Z I A Z T P Y G E K N
C C B R B L U P G U W O
U Y J X D F N L O C C T
E E C Y D A A X Y A N S
Y K J U L E M Y K I T G
A R A O X C P M O R A N
R U P B T O A M T O S I
A T A Y Y T O N C R O K
K G N A C I A M A J E D
N S A E D L K W T D S H
A J S P A I N Y A Y A J
```

Madrid

Kingston

Tokyo

Ankara

Cairo

Ottawa

CANADA

Egypt

Turkey

Spain

JAMAICA

Japan

日本

Word connections

Find a word that can go after the word on the left and in front of the word on the right to make two new words.

AIR .... ABLE

SEARCH .... HOUSE

WOOD .... MARK

SWIM .... CASE

BASE .... ROOM

BUS .... PORT

SECOND .... RAIL

Long flight

Jack is flying from Melbourne, Australia, to Boston, USA, stopping off in San Francisco on the way. Use the information below to calculate what the time and date will be in Boston when he arrives.

Jack's flight leaves Melbourne at 8:00 p.m. on Friday, April 30th.

Boston is 14 hours behind Melbourne, so when it's the middle of the morning in Boston, it's already night time in Melbourne.

The flight from San Francisco to Boston takes 6 hours.

The flight from Melbourne to San Francisco takes 17 hours.

Jack's stop in San Francisco is 3 hours.

ANSWER . . . .

Suitcase fifteens

Label these suitcases with the numbers 1 to 9 so that each row, column and diagonal line of three adds up to 15. The first three numbers have already been filled in for you.

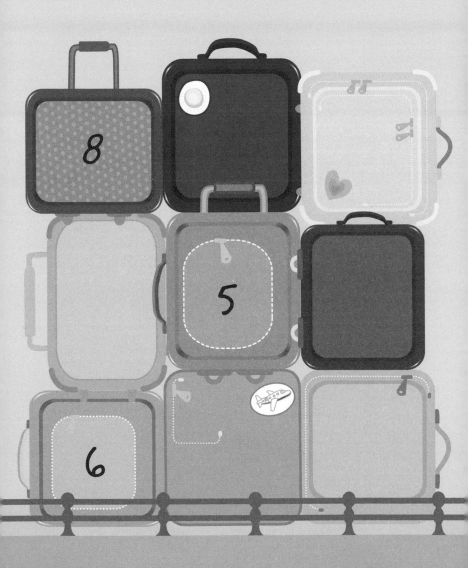

In the hangar

Three planes are parked in the airport's hangar. Following the clues below, can you find out the pilot of each plane, the day they arrived, and where each one will fly to next? Fill in your answers on the chart.

Arrived	Pilot	Plane	Destination
Tuesday			
Wednesday			
Thursday			

1. Lionel arrived some time after the pilot heading to Paris.
2. Pegasus landed at the airport on Tuesday.
3. Elsa is not going to Vienna.
4. Claude flies Skylark, and arrived later in the week than the pilot who is heading to Dublin.
5. Hermes did not land at the airport on Thursday.

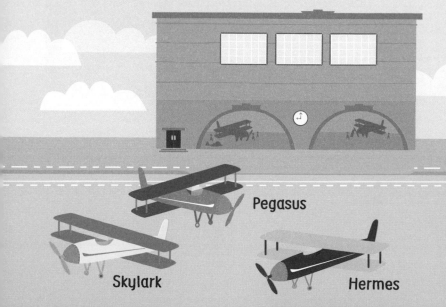

Pegasus

Skylark

Hermes

Packing list code

Your friend is taking you on a surprise trip. The exotic destination is hidden in this packing list. Can you find out where it is? Clue: look carefully at the number next to each item.

What you'll need:
1 passport
2 or 3 books
4 snorkels
5 shirts
2 sunhats
1 guidebook
3 beach towels
5 bottles of sunscreen

ANSWER ....

Planes of symmetry

On the grids below, the dotted lines are mirrors. Draw the reflection of each plane in the correct place on the other half of its grid.

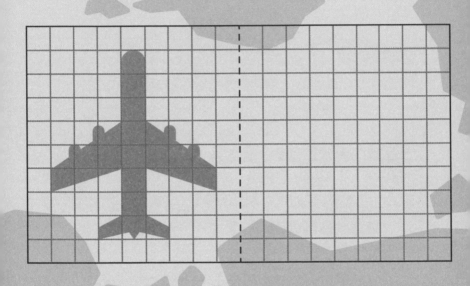

Stamp designing

Use the blank stamps to create your own designs,
inspired by places all over the world.

Flight grid

Plot the coordinates below on this chart, then join them in order. What shape do they make? The first number in each pair shows how many squares to count across from 0. The second shows how many to count up or down.

(−4, −2) (1, 3) (0, 4) (4, 4) (4, 0)
(3, 1) (−2, −4) (−2, −2) (−4, −2)

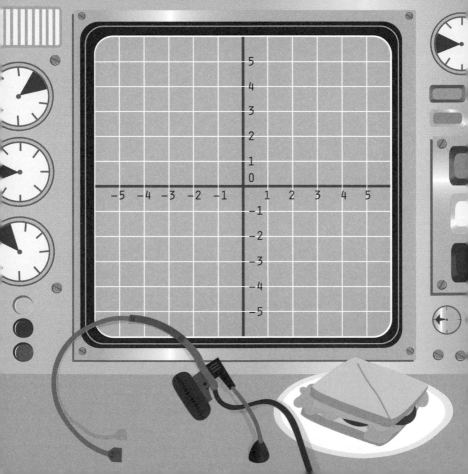

Which gate?

Starting from each gate, follow the trails to find out which one you need to catch the plane.

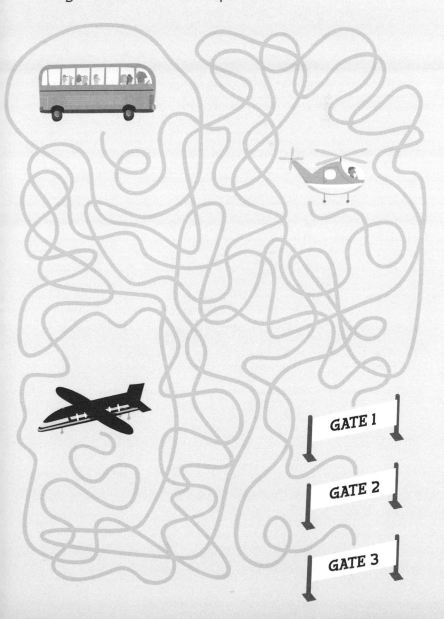

X-ray vision

This suitcase is passing through the x-ray machine at the security desk. Draw what else is inside it.

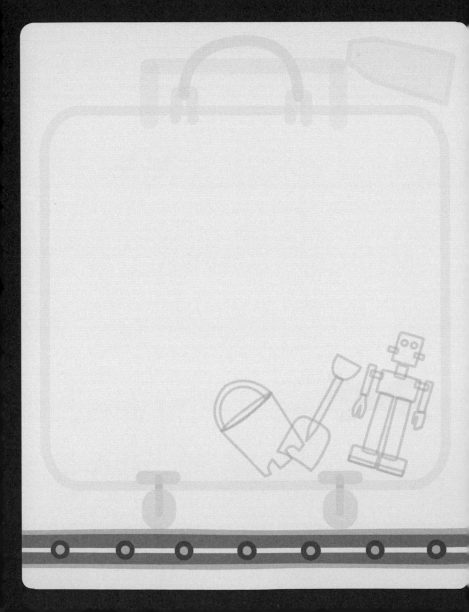

Runway numbers

Can you help the pilot find the right terminal? At each turn
he must take the runway whose question gives the lowest
answer. Circle the correct terminal.

72-58=?

13+14=?

100÷4=?

5x7=?

28÷2=?

17+12=?

63-26=?

39÷3=?

16x4=?

26+14=?

19+17=?

29-16=?

3x9=?

4x8=?

15x3=?

64-49=?

4x6=?

32+27=?

T1   T2   T3   T4   T5

The captain

Doodle a face on the captain and a flight badge on his hat.

Bird's-eye view

Look carefully at the airport buildings below. Which view would you see if you were looking at them from directly above?

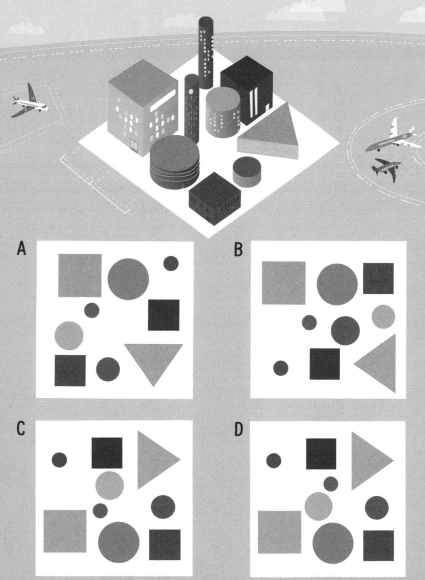

A

B

C

D

Planes grid

In the picture below, draw around the two groups of six planes that match the groups shown on the right.

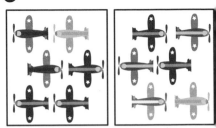

Cloudy landing

Guide the plane safely between the clouds to the runway.

Money matters

1. Alice and Emma flew from London to Sydney with six other friends, and changed their money at the airport. Alice changed 60 pounds, and got 135 dollars in return. How many dollars did Emma get for 100 pounds?

ANSWER ....

2. When they arrived, they all bought same-priced ice creams, and the bill was 17 dollars. Alice didn't know how much one ice cream was, but instantly knew the bill was wrong. How did she know this?

Plane doodles

Add windows, doors and a cockpit to these planes, then design patterns and airline logos along their sides.

Weather doodle

Doodle lots of clouds in the sky around this plane, then add rain, lightning, sunshine or rainbows.

Conveyor belt

Study the eight toy models below for 30 seconds, then cover them up and write down as many as you can remember in the spaces below.

....

....

....

....

Draw an airship

Follow the steps below to draw an airship, then fill the sky with lots more of them.

 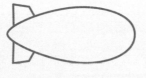 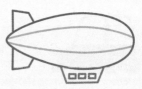

1. Draw this shape for a gas bag.

2. Add tail fins.

3. Add these lines, a cabin and windows.

Plane search

Find the plane words below hidden in the grid. They may be written in any direction.

```
E S U F R U N W A Y A N
T G R E D D U R A I G P
E Y A W E K A T R A W O
R P I N A I R P N U A R
M R F O F F O W A S E T
I O U A A R T G I L T I
N F S I T G O F L N O P
A F E N I G N E R I G K
L R L N I L P E B B R C
G P A W T O N G O A N O
A R G E R I W C H C A C
O B E P F F O E K A T E
```

wing
rudder
terminal
cockpit
engine
cabin
airport
propeller
runway
takeoff
fuselage

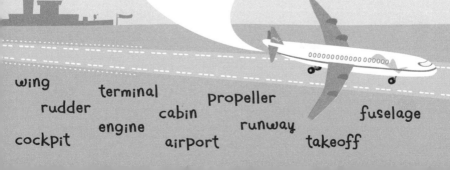

Pilot's perspective

Draw what you think the pilot can see from the cockpit.

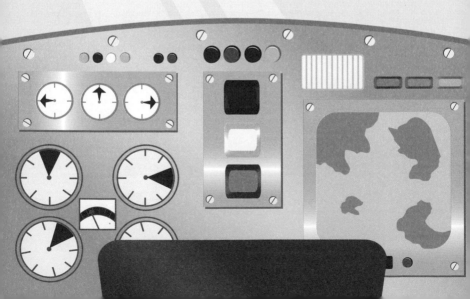

Flying home

Guide the pilot of this plane from airport to airport, back home. Avoid the red airports, because they have no fuel.

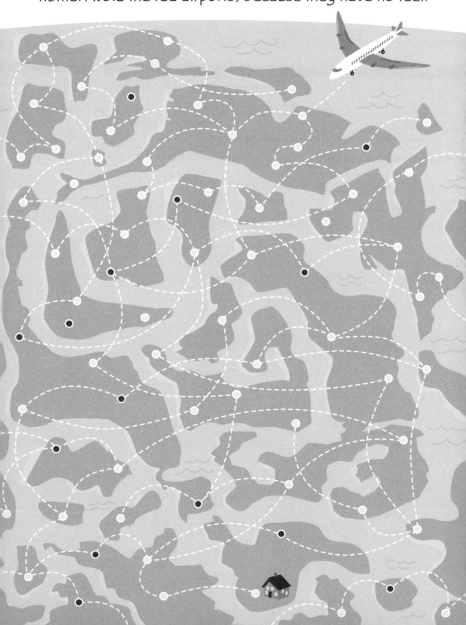

Giant plane

Draw another plane on the grid, exactly the same shape but twice as big. The first part has been done for you.

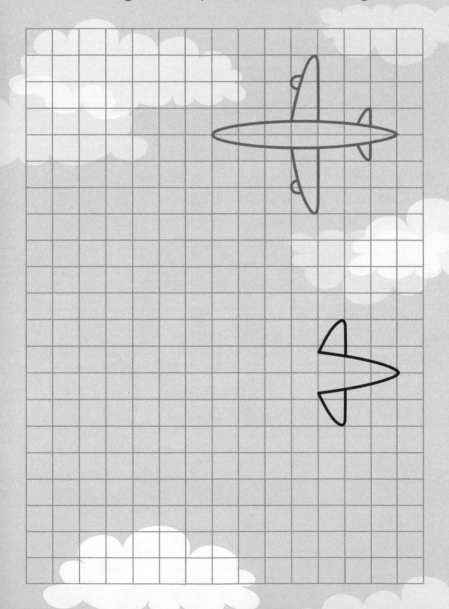

Foods of the world

Draw lines matching each dish to the country that is famous for serving it.

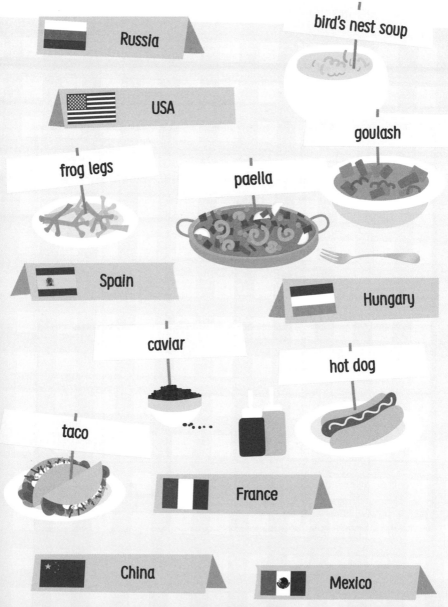

Flight sudoku

The grid below is made up of six blocks, each made up of six squares. Fill in the blank squares so that every row, column and block contains all six letters of the word FLIGHT.

	I	T	H		F
		G			I
T				H	L
H	L				
G			I		
		L	G	F	H

Flight attendant

Doodle a face on the flight attendant and a design on her hat.

Passenger differences

Spot ten differences between the groups of passengers sitting on either side of the aisle.

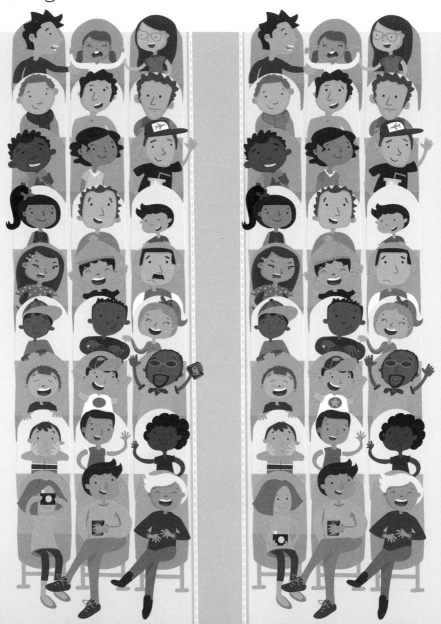

Flight quiz

1) A drone is an aircraft that does not have...
a) wings?   b) a pilot?   c) an engine?

2) Is it easier for planes to take off:
into the wind **or** with the wind behind them?

3) What was the first and only passenger plane to fly faster than the speed of sound?
a) Concorde   b) Boeing 747   c) Airbus A330

4) On a plane cruising at high altitude, food doesn't taste as nice. True or false?

5) What is a plane's speed measured in?
a) air miles   b) light years   c) knots

6) What is used to test a plane's design?
a) air bridge   b) wind tunnel   c) windsock

7) Who was the first woman to fly solo across the Atlantic: Ellen McArthur **or** Amelia Earhart?

Plane parts

Circle the group of parts that can be put together to make up the plane shown on the right.

A
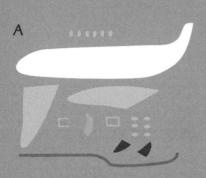

B
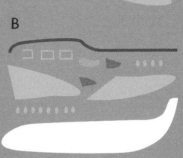

C
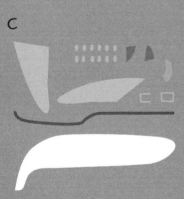

D
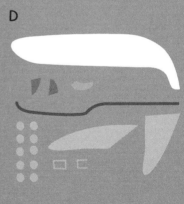

E
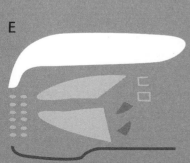

F

Crossword 3

Use the clues below to put the correct words into the grid.

Across

1. What spins around to make some planes go (9)
6. Towards the sky (2)
7. Portable lamp; Chinese _____ (7)
8. Opposite of 6 across (4)
9. Browned bread (5)
10. Insect; move through the air (3)
11. Sit on the fronts of your legs (5)
15. Once a year (6)
16. Charlie and Willy Wonka flew in the Great Glass _____ (8)

Down

1. A plane driver (5)
2. Possess (3)
3. Throw out; bail out (5)
4. Come down to earth (4)
5. Where planes take off from (6)
10. A fish's limb (3)
11. Stringed toy for the sky (4)
12. Border, rim, verge (4)
13. Hot liquid rock (4)
14. How birds move their wings (4)

Postcards

Spot ten differences between
these two postcards.

Suitcase search

Your suitcase is somewhere in
this jumble – it's big, round and
green. Find it, then weave
your way through the
stacks of cases
to collect it.

WAY IN

Carousel confusion

Guide the luggage along the carousel to the people waiting.

Answers

1. Packing jumble:
Snorkel and mask

2. Key match-up: B and F

3. From the air:

4. Forward and back:
1. Green 2. Yellow 3. Green

5. Time zones:

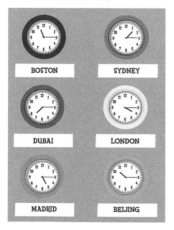

6. Air quiz:
1) b   2) c   3) b   4) a   5) c   6) True (to reduce the chances of the food making all of them ill)   7) a

7. Parking space:

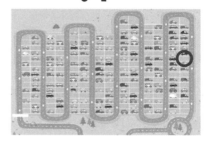

8. Counting planes: 13 planes

9. Loading luggage:

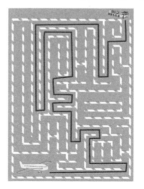

10. Anna's alarm:

Answers

12. Bags and cases:
3 red, 1 blue, 2 green,
3 orange, 1 yellow

13. Symbol sudoku:

14. Flag mix-up:

Jamaica

France

New Zealand

Germany

United States

Mexico

15. Lost luggage:

16. Departures:
1. DFG175   2. 09:05

17. Flight plan:

18. Planes puzzle: Day 13

19. Cross sum:

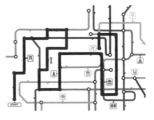

20. Hotel hurry:

21. Gridlock:
20% blue, 25% red, 50% green

Answers

C

26. What am I?:

1. a river 2. a cloud 3. a clock
4. breath 5. an envelope
6. an arrow 7. a stamp

27. Excess baggage:

28. Globe words: 25

BONE**CHINA**DOLLNARNIA
SWEDENRUSHERRORGREASE
CREATEISLAND**EGYPTCANADA**TAPED
CHILLYCOLONY**POLANDNORWAY**PANIC
PLUMP**ROMANIA**RIVERVILLAIN**COSTARICA**
BIRDLAND**TURKEY**NATIVECASHEWAGILITYAGO
TROPICOCEAN**MADAGASCARBRAZIL**INCASON
MAGENTA**IRELAND**BANANA**NETHERLANDS**POT
JAMAICAKNOWNIN**JAPAN**HUNGRYSAXON**CHILE**
PORTUGALVENT**FIJIRUSSIA**GONEPROVINCE
ALMONDPACIFIC**PERU**SEAT**ICELAND**WAIT
BEAROUT**FRANCE**LILLIPUTRAFT**ITALY**
NEVERLAND**INDIA**GUITARMEXCO
TWOMAN**GERMANY**COLDER

29. Plane scramble:

autopilot, cockpit, landing gear,
stewardess, passenger, captain

30. Flight timeline:

1. Kite 2. Hot-air balloon
3. Glider 4. Plane
5. Helicopter 6. Space Shuttle

31. Stunt planes:

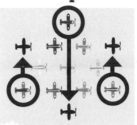

32. Crossword 1:

33. Air race:

1. *Phantom*
2. *Lightning*
3. *Rainbow*
4. *Pinky*
5. *Camouflage*

34. Aircraft search:

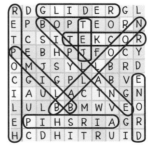

Answers

35. Cities in the sky:
LONDON BERLIN MOSCOW
SYDNEY ATHENS LISBON

36. Travel times:
Longest: 2   Shortest: 4

37. Lines and dots:

38. Hot-air balloon:
Hot: 7   Air: 10

39. Around the airport:

40. Find your bag:

41. Landmarks quiz:
1) c 2) false 3) b 4) a 5) a 6) c

42. Plane mechanic:
Plane 4

44. Flight chart:
Boeing 737: 7   Learjet 60: 5
Airbus A380: 6   Beechcraft 1900: 2
Antonov AN-158: 5

46. Earth splitting:

47. Crossnumber:

1	2	1	5	2		1	3
0				8	0		6
1	9	4	5				0
	.		0	0	7		
	7				4	5	6
1	5		1	4	7		0
2				1			7
3	6	6		1	9	8	4

49. True or false?:
1. False 2. True 3. True 4. True
5. False 6. True 7. True

Answers

51. On autopilot:

52. Radio alphabet:

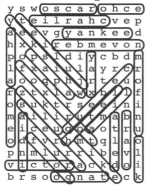

54. Ground control:

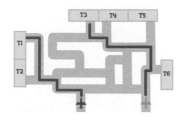

55. Plane designs:
Three planes left blank

56. Runway rules:
Runway 1 - C
Runway 2 - D

57. Stunt search:

58. Birds in words:

1. The usual bat Ross uses is broken.

2. The republic ran everything after that.

3. Sam learned to ski with his parents.

4. The kangaroo kicked his rival hard.

5. Alice climbed the path awkwardly in her heels.

6. The sea gleamed in the sunshine.

7. We can either go West, or keep going North.

8. The man who built this wall owns the land.

59. Flying jumble: 9

60. Crossword 2:

Answers

61. Flags scramble:

 Italy

 Brazil

 Switzerland

 South Africa

 Australia

Canada

63. Hidden picture:

64. Capital cities:

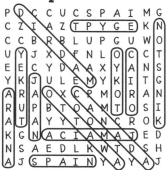

Canada - Ottawa
Egypt - Cairo
Spain - Madrid
Turkey - Ankara
Jamaica - Kingston
Japan - Tokyo

65. Word connections:

1. port 2. light 3. land 4. suit
5. ball 6. pass 7. hand

66. Long flight:

8:00 a.m. Saturday, May 1st

67. Suitcase fifteens:

68. In the hangar:

Arrived	Pilot	Plane	Destination
Tuesday	Elsa	Pegasus	Paris
Wednesday	Lionel	Hermes	Dublin
Thursday	Claude	Skylark	Vienna

69. Packing list code:

Portugal

70. Planes of symmetry:

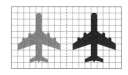

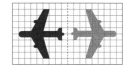

72. Flight grid:

73. Which gate?: Gate 3

Captain's report

Finish filling in the captain's report on the screen below, noting down any extra details of interest. If you're on a plane, you could use your own flight details.

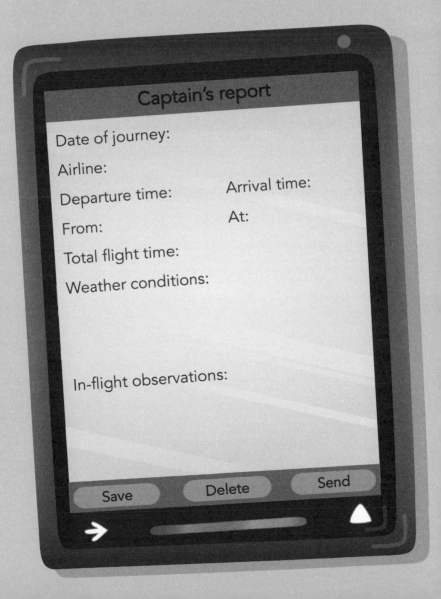

Captain's report

Date of journey:

Airline:

Departure time: Arrival time:

From: At:

Total flight time:

Weather conditions:

In-flight observations:

Save   Delete   Send

Arrivals

Use the arrivals board to answer the questions below.

Time	From	Flight	Gate
	ARRIVALS		T1
04:20	PRAGUE	KSD236	09
04:25	TOKYO	LCT957	16
04:25	CAPE TOWN	ENC677	23
04:30	HANOI	FLP844	02
04:55	STOCKHOLM	WMG206	18
05:05	BOSTON	MAS954	31
05:10	BUDAPEST	LFW703	29
05:15	ATHENS	AXF686	03
05:20	MELBOURNE	FLK206	05
05:35	HELSINKI	HHT389	14
05:45	BEIJING	DFG634	12
06:05	MOSCOW	UPL842	17

1. Megan's flight was due to arrive 35 minutes before the flight at gate 14, but is delayed by an hour and a half. What time will it arrive now?

ANSWER ....

2. When Phil took off, it was 00:15 at this airport. His flight takes four hours and 50 minutes. Where has he been?

ANSWER ....

Answers

75. Runway numbers:

77. Bird's-eye view: C

78. Planes grid:

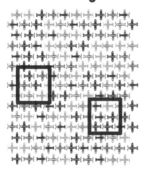

79. Cloudy landing:

80. Money matters:
1. 225 coins
2. 17 can't be divided by 8

85. Plane search:

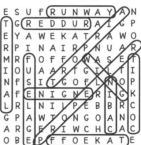

```
E S U f R U N W A Y A N
T G R E D D U R A I G P
E Y A W E K A T R A W O
R P I N A I R P N U A R
M R f O f f O W A S E T
I O U A A R T G I L f I
N f S I T G O f L N O P
A f E N I G N E R I G K
L R L N I P E B B R C
G P A W T O N G O A N O
A R G f R I W C H C A C
O B E P f f O E K A T E
```

87. Flying home:

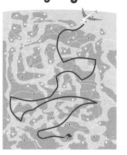

88. Giant plane:

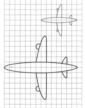

89. Foods of the world:
Russia - caviar; USA - hot dog;
Spain - paella; France - frog legs;
Mexico - taco; Hungary - goulash;
China - bird's nest soup

90. Flight sudoku:

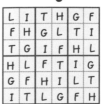

L	I	T	H	G	F
F	H	G	L	T	I
T	G	I	F	H	L
H	L	F	T	I	G
G	F	H	I	L	T
I	T	L	G	F	H

Answers

92. Passenger differences:

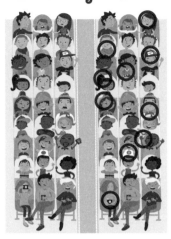

93. Flight quiz:
1. b 2. into the wind 3. a 4. True
5. c 6. b 7. Amelia Earhart

94. Plane parts: C

95. Crossword 3:

96. Postcards:

97. Suitcase search:

98. Carousel confusion:

100. Arrivals:
1. 6:30   2. Boston

With thanks to Candice Whatmore and Lizzie Barber

First published in 2016 by Usborne Publishing Ltd, 83–85 Saffron Hill, London ECIN 8RT, England.